If I Could Ask Jesus

Endorsements

Donna Wyland's *If I Could Ask Jesus* is a wonderful foundation building book for little people. With poetic rhyme and childlike imagination, Donna communicates the truth about angels. The illustrations are precious!

—**Shelley Pierce**, author, *The Wish I Wished Last Night*

Do you have questions you want to ask Jesus when you get to heaven? In *If I Could Ask Jesus*, author Donna Wyland asks those questions, seeing the world through the eyes of a child. You will enjoy reading this book with your little one, and it is a great conversation starter to ask your little one, "If you could ask Jesus a question, what would it be?"

—**Michelle S. Lazurek**, author of *Uniquely You*

Author Donna Wyland has written a picture book that will not only delight children with its lilting rhyme and charming illustrations but will also give voice to the valid questions children may have about God's angels.

—**MaryAnn Diorio**, PhD., Author of *The Italian Chronicles Trilogy*

Delightful and heartwarming! *If I Could Ask Jesus* is a book you will want to read over and over to children of all ages. The thoughtful questions and beautiful illustrations stir a child's curiosity, encourages them to talk to GOD, and helps them begin to grow in relationship with Our Creator. A truly beautiful book!

Janice LaVore-Fletcher, Founder and President, Christian Coach Institute

If I Could Ask Jesus

Elk Lake
PUBLISHING, INC.
PLYMOUTH, MASSACHUSETTS

by Donna Wyland
art by Lynne Marie Davis

Cover Design: Lynne Davis
Interior Design: Lynne Davis, Cheryl L. Childers
Editor(s): Deb Haggerty
Published in Association with Hartline Literary Agency and Sally Apokedak Agency

PUBLISHED BY: Elk Lake Publishing, Inc., 35 Dogwood Dr., Plymouth, MA 02360, 2018

Library Cataloging Data

Names: Wyland, Donna with Davis, Lynne (Donna Wyland with Lynne Davis)
If I Could Ask Jesus | Donna Wyland with Lynne Davis
32 p. 25.4cm × 20.32cm (10 in × 8 in.)
Description: Children's curiosity questions about heaven and angels.
Identifiers: ISBN-13: 978-1-948888-16-5 (trade) | 978-1-948888-17-2 (POD) | 978-1-948888-18-9 (e-book.)
Key Words: Heaven, Angels, Children, Kids, Family, Bedtime,
LCCN: 2018948271 Fiction

Dedication

For Bentley...
Donna Wyland

For Bill and all our children...
Lynne Marie Davis

If I could ask Jesus some questions out loud,

I'd ask what it's like to live high in a cloud.

I'd ask if His heavenly house is like mine,

Or if it's surrounded

by angels divine.

I'd ask Him how angels grow wings on their backs.

Do they have skateboards and scooters and snacks?

Just how do they sleep without bending their wings?

Do they fold up like boxes that hold special things?

I'd ask Him if angels read books, sing, and play,

And when they are taught just the right way to pray.

Do angels get bruises and scrapes on their knees?

Do they eat broccoli covered with cheese?

I'd ask Him if angels have feelings that hurt,

And if their white robes get all covered with dirt.

Do angels have someone to tuck them in tight?

Do they get scared when the day turns to night?

I'd ask Him if I have an angel down here,

And though I can't see it, I'd ask if it's near.

I'd thank Him for keeping me safe every day,

Then I'd tell Him goodnight till the next time I pray.

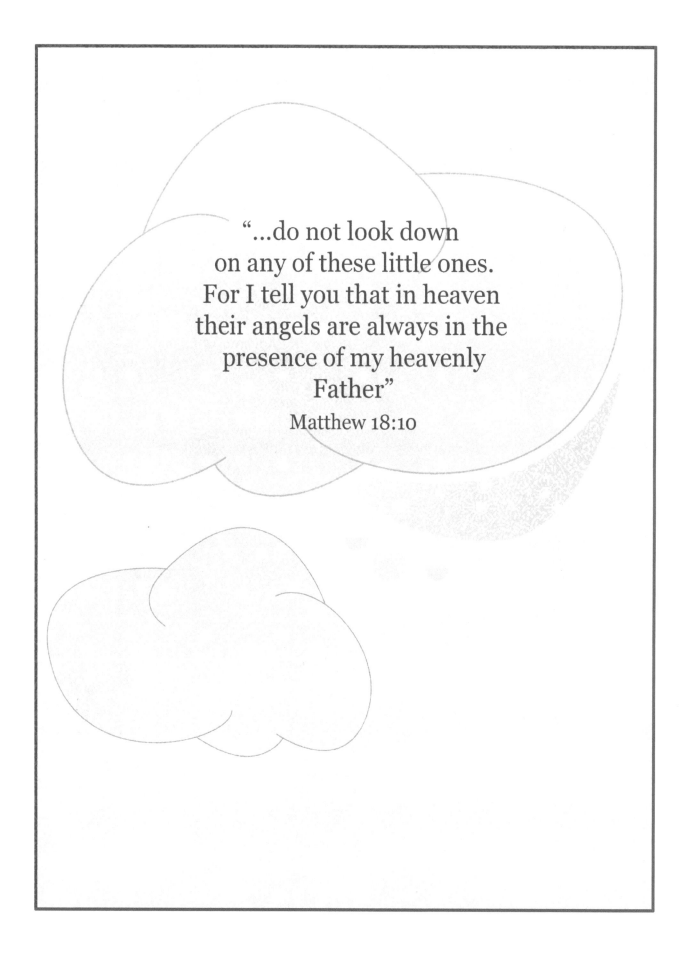

"...do not look down
on any of these little ones.
For I tell you that in heaven
their angels are always in the
presence of my heavenly
Father"

Matthew 18:10

About the Author

Donna Wyland is an Award-winning author, ghostwriter and coach who has been writing since her first diary entry at the age of nine.

Influenced most by Dr. Seuss, Donna enjoys the creative process of combining rhythm and rhyme to produce children's books that entertain as well as inform. She is a certified speaker through CLASS (Christian Leaders, Authors and Speakers Service) and enjoys meeting and talking with children on school visits.

Donna is the author of the bestselling picture book, *Your Home in Heaven*, and has had numerous children's poems published in various magazines. She is also a contributing writer for several collections of poetry and personal essays. Donna is currently working on a series of rhyming board books and a picture book titled, "Everything Jesus."

Social Media links:
Facebook – http://www.facebook.com/donna.wyland
Pinterest - http://www.pinterest.com/donnawyland
LinkedIn - http://www.linkedin.com/in/donna-wyland
Email - donna@donnawyland.com

About the Artist

Lynne Marie Davis is an artist and art teacher who loves declaring the goodness of God through her art and illustrations as well as her teaching workshops. She resides a stone's throw from stunning in the North Georgia mountains with her dreamy husband Bill and their cat Tux.

CPSIA information can be obtained
at www.ICGtesting.com
Printed in the USA
BVHW021043110620
581241BV00005B/91